NICOLA DAVIES

BEE BOY

AND THE MOONFLOWERS

ILLUSTRATIONS MAX LOW

For Naomi and Sue with love

Bee Boy and the Moonflowers
Published in Great Britain in 2018
by Graffeg Limited.

Written by Nicola Davies
copyright © 2018.
Illustrated by Max Low
copyright © 2018.
Designed and produced by Graffeg
Limited copyright © 2018.

Graffeg Limited, 24 Stradey Park
Business Centre, Mwrwg Road,
Llangennech, Llanelli, Carmarthenshire
SA14 8YP Wales UK
Tel 01554 824000 www.graffeg.com

Nicola Davies is hereby identified as the
author of this work in accordance with
section 77 of the Copyrights, Designs and
Patents Act 1988.

A CIP Catalogue record for this book is
available from the British Library.

ISBN 9781910862513

1 2 3 4 5 6 7 8 9

NICOLA DAVIES
BEE BOY
AND THE MOONFLOWERS

ILLUSTRATIONS MAX LOW

GRAFFEG

BEE BOY
AND THE MOONFLOWERS

Beyond the little green eye of the oasis, the land rose, bleak and red into rocky peaks. Even now, so close to sunset, Azin saw how the heat bent the light, making the air shimmer with the illusion of water, so that the mountains glowed like bloodied teeth against a silver sea. Up there, heat was a life-sucking vampire, and water came in violent flash floods.

He looked around him, at his family, his mother, father, his older brothers, lying on the floor of the tent. Only the healing strength of Silver Honey could save them. Only bees that gathered the nectar of Moonflowers from the highest mountain ridges could make Silver Honey. So somebody *had* to take the bees to find the Moonflowers and the only person not too sick or too old was Azin. Never in his life had Azin *had* to do anything. Somebody older than him had always done it for him.

His grandmother touched his forehead, her hand light as a leaf.

"It's time to go," she said.

Azin nodded and tried to feel brave. All he felt was small.

Hennu, the family's oldest camel, the only camel who wasn't as sick as the people, rose with Azin on her back. Even now he hoped his grandmother would tell him to get down, that she'd go into the mountains instead. But she didn't.

"Head east," she told him, "keep to the shade of the canyons, until you see clouds, then up to the high ridges. Listen to the bees, Azin, they will tell you when they smell Moonflowers."

"I don't think I can do this, Granny." Azin almost wailed.

"Yes you can! Trust yourself!"

Azin turned Hennu quickly, so as not to show his tears, and let himself be carried away. He did

not look back until the tent beside the oasis was
no more than a pale smudge in the darkness.

A crescent moon rose and sliced between
the peaks, and the stars blazed out. Night was
when the family travelled to find the next bloom
of flowers, the next grove of pomegranates or
almonds for their bees. Usually Azin slept on the
back of his father's camel, lulled by the rhythmic
rock and tilt of the animal's stride. But now he had
to stay awake and think: *he had ten days of water;
that gave him five days to find the flowers and five
days to travel back.* He stared up at the stars, and
thought, *it's impossible.*

Morning came scorching over the horizon,
curves of wind-carved rock were all around and
the oasis was far behind. As the sun got high, they
rested in the deep shadows under the overhangs.
Hennu would not need water on the journey, but
she did need food. Azin measured out a small
ration of dried peas for her, then dripped sugared

water into the hives to nourish the bees. He ate only the skin of a date, as his grandmother had told him to, and saved the flesh for tomorrow. His belly growled and the task ahead of him was far too big. He knew he was too small to match it.

Three more nights passed under the stars with travelling and three days went by in the shade, full with worrying. Hennu was good-natured enough for a camel, but she wasn't much company compared with five brothers. The canyons twisted and turned so it was hard to keep to a direction. The maze of rock was more and more like a trap. Azin wondered what he would do if he did not find Moonflowers in time.

Then, at dawn on the fifth day, the narrow canyon opened out, revealing a wadi at its end and a high ridge above, veiled in dense, grey cloud! Perhaps up there Moonflowers were already blooming. But Azim hesitated; with rain on the peaks above, the wadi could fill with water in

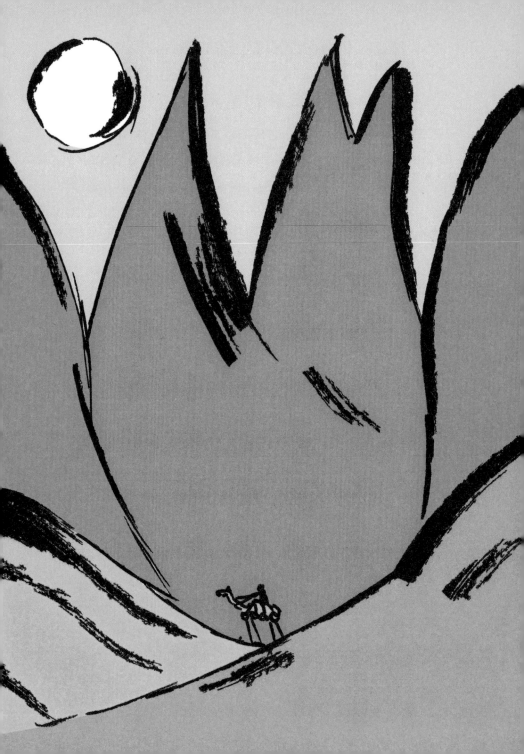

minutes. What should he do? He paced about, not wanting to make a decision. By the time he realised there *was* no choice, he'd wasted hours.

Up the wadi they went, but Azin had delayed too long. Lightning split the clouds and the air cracked with thunder. Hennu refused to go on and as Azin slid from her back to try to pull her onwards, another sound drowned out the camel's protests, a deep rumbling like a monster clearing its throat, a flood! Azin pulled the camel sideways, to an outcrop of rock that rose above the wadi floor. He flung his arms around her neck and prepared to die as the flood of water and rocks rose round them.

As fast as it had come, the flood was gone. The sky above was blue again, leaving a grumble of thunder, no more than a camel's indigestion. They were alive, but Hennu was bleeding from a wound on her right foreleg and all but two of the beehives were full of water and small, drowned bodies. Azin wanted to sit down and cry, but there was no one to dry his tears. So he straightened his shoulders instead, bound his camel's wounds, refilled the goatskins from the pools the flood had left behind, and set off up the wadi. At least now they had replenished their water supply they had enough for ten days again, and, somewhere up above, the rain could be bringing Moonflowers into bloom.

The ridge, when they reached it, was more a plateau, cut with deep ravines. The air shimmered in the fierce heat. Azin shaded his eyes and stared. Was that a haze of green and silver Moonflowers in the distance, or just a mirage? There was only one way to find out, but every time they got closer, a ravine cut their path and sent them on a long detour.

The bees seemed certain however. The two remaining hives began to make a sound Azin had never heard bees make before, a kind of thrumming chant, as if the insects' wings were beating in unison against the walls of their prison. Was this the sign Grandmother had told him

to listen for? He couldn't be sure. He decided he must get closer so he could really see the flowers, before letting the bees out to forage.

They pressed on through the afternoon, ravines always keeping them from progressing in a straight line. The horizon still shimmered with a mysterious silver that might, or might not, be Moonflowers. But Azin could endure the bees strange chanting no longer. He took down one of the hives, the one with the red door, placed it on a rock and let the bees out. They took a moment to fly round, to see where their front door had opened, and then they streamed towards the distant shine of green and silver. Azin knew that if he moved their hive now, the bees would not find their way home. All he could do was wait. He unsaddled Hennu, and sat with the other hive in the small shade her body offered, calming the bees with an extra ration of sugared water.

Azin woke as the sun was sinking, to find a bee on his nose. He caught her gently in his cupped hands and placed his eye to the crack between his fingers. Her pollen baskets shone with a pearly gleam, like powdered moonlight, quite unlike the yellow of normal pollen! That *must* have come from Moonflowers! He released the bee and lifted the lid of the hive enough to peep inside. Silver Honey was unmistakable, it glinted like quicksilver in the waxy cells. But there was barely enough to wet a fingertip. What was worse, the hive was almost empty. Barely a handful of bees had returned. Perhaps the journey to the Moonflowers had been just too long.

There was nothing to do but leave the red-doored hive behind, in case the bees returned, and try to get closer to the Moonflowers by morning. Azin loaded Hennu and set off, determined to reach the flowers. They didn't stop all night, they didn't stop at dawn, or when the sun climbed in the sky. The pale shine on the horizon grew and grew. It changed from a vague, shimmering silver,

to a definite, glowing white. From a streak of
colour to billowing blossoms.

At last, Azin stood in a sea of flowers that
shone as if all the stars in heaven had fallen
and dissolved in all the pearls of the ocean. Even
Hennu was impressed, and grazed carefully
around them on green shoots of new grass.

Joyfully, Azin opened the last hive, the one with
the blue door. The bees leapt into the air, wild with
delight to be surrounded by flowers whose scent
had been calling to them. Within minutes, they
were flying back to the hive in their dozens, loaded
with pollen, their small bodies full to bursting
with the magical nectar. Perhaps they *would* make
enough Silver Honey to cure his whole family!

But Azin's delight did not last. From nowhere,
birds appeared. Not just any birds, but bee-
eaters, with their long beaks and agile flight, the
colours of their feathers flashing in the sun. They
began gobbling up his bees, five, ten, twenty in
their beaks at once. Furious, Azin sent a hail of

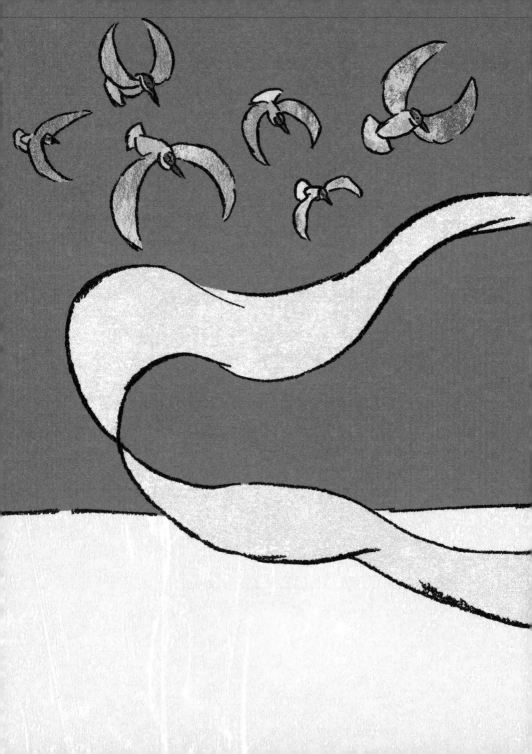

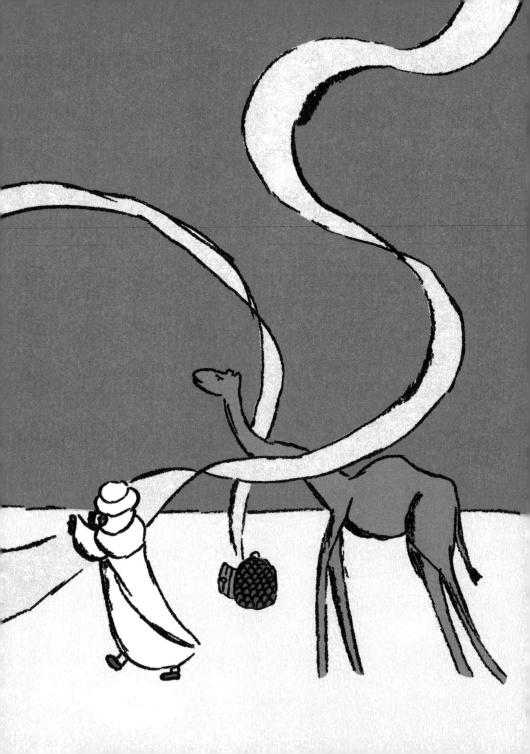

pebbles towards the birds to scare them off. They retreated, and wheeled round in a small, tight flock. Now Azin was too angry to stop. He kept throwing, until one bird was hit and fell to the ground behind a boulder.

He ran to the place to chase the other bee eaters away, but what he saw made him drop to his knees. The birds had come to roost in the long silky fur of a great she-bear. They looked out as if from the safety of their own nests. In her huge paws, the bear held the injured bird and fat tears rolled down her furry cheeks. As Azin watched, the injured bird changed. Its wings vanished and hands appeared in their place and a child's eyes looked out at him.

"I'm dying! I'm dying!" the little one cried.

Azin was horrified. He raced to the blue-doored hive, and while the furious bees stung his arms and face, he broke a little of the newly filled comb and ran with it to the bear. The honey trickled like melted moon from the yellow cells of wax.

"This is why I came here," Azin cried, "to collect this honey to cure my family. It will heal all hurts."

The bear looked at Azin, its tawny eyes seemed to look right into him. And then it spoke, with a girl's voice!

"Are you a sorcerer?" the creature asked.

Azin shook his head.

"I'm just a beekeeper," he replied, "but that is very special honey."

"It seems," said the bear, "that I have no choice but to trust you."

She held out the dying bird-child and, very gently, Azin trickled a tiny bit of pearly honey into its mouth. Its little tongue licked hungrily, like a flame at a dry twig, and its remaining feathers shivered. A moment later and all trace of bird-ness was gone, and all hurt too: a little boy sat smiling in the bear's lap.

The bear turned her head and fixed Azin once more with her deep eyes.

"Do you perhaps have a little more honey?" she asked.

Azin could not refuse. His guilt over the child he had so nearly killed would not let him. As night fell, time and time again he went back to the hive, until ten children with dark silky hair and big brown eyes were curled up to sleep in the fur of their guardian, the bear.

"They have been under an enchantment," the bear explained, shifting her paws a little to make one of the children more comfortable, "we believed the spell would only break with death. But your honey has proved us wrong."

"Are you not also under an enchantment?" Azin asked the bear.

Once again the bear looked keenly at him and replied, "My enchantment is a very big one, it would use all your honey to change it. Besides," the bear continued, "when we begin our journey out of these mountains, I must carry all my brothers and sisters."

Azin crept away and fell into an exhausted slumber by his hive and his camel. He dreamed of the Silver Honey that the bees would make tomorrow, enough to heal his family *and* the bear, no matter how great her enchantment.

But as the sun rose, Azin saw that the Moonflowers had withered in the night! His heart stopped in his chest. A tiny piece of comb was all that was left, and he realised that eight days of water for one person was less than one day of water for eleven people and a bear. He would not be able to take even this tiny thimbleful of Silver Honey home!

When he told the bear, however, she seemed unworried.

"Let us begin the journey anyway!" she said, "Something good may happen along the way. It may rain, for instance."

The bear's words were so hopeful, and the children riding on her broad back so cheerful, that Azin felt better. He shared the water and the last of the dates with the children and the bear, and fed Hennu. Then, in spite of the heat and the lack of water, they set off together, with the blue-doored hive closed up and loaded on the camel's back.

The bear was right. It did rain. Not a great storm to fill a wadi in moments, but a little grey cloud that formed over their heads like a parasol and rained onto them.

"There," said the bear, "another day of water."

The distance around the ravines seemed somehow to have shrunk. They reached the red-doored hive in just a few hours.

"Perhaps," suggested the bear, "you should look inside?"

Azin lifted the lid of the hive. It wasn't full by any means, but it wasn't empty either. Many more of the bees had returned and must have brought with them pearly nectar from Moonflowers, because the inside of the little hive glowed with Silver Honey.

"If only I could get this back to my family!" Azin cried.

"I don't see why not," said the bear.

But no more good things happened. The day was exceedingly hot and there was no more rain. That night it was so cold their teeth chattered as they walked and the sun caught them as they travelled down the wadi, before they could reach the shade of the canyon at the bottom. Even Hennu suffered from the heat and thirst, and groaned loudly with every footstep.

"Well," said the bear, "as good things are not happening on their own, we must make them happen."

She held up a square of cloth and they all huddled miserably in its meagre shade.

"Silver Honey alone is not enough to *break* my enchantment," said the bear, "but you, Azin, can add an ingredient that will make *change*."

Azin was astonished.

"What could I possibly add?" he said.

"Do you trust me, Azin?" said the bear.

Azin looked at the bear.

"Yes," he answered, somewhat to his surprise, "I do trust you!"

"Then give me the last of the honey from the blue-doored hive and I will take the red-doored hive to your family. Then I will send you help."

"What about your brothers and sisters?" Azin replied.

"If you can trust yourself," said the bear slowly, "I can trust you to keep them safe until help comes."

Azin felt as if the glow of the Silver Honey had entered into his heart with the bear's words. He nodded, then took the last bit of silvery comb from the blue-doored hive and put it on the bear's tongue. The square of cloth fluttered in a sudden breeze, and where the bear had been, a golden eagle stretched its wings. It took off with the little red-doored hive grasped tightly in its talons and disappeared into the west.

At first, the children cried, but Azin told them stories and made them laugh. He gave them each the stone of a date to suck on, and told them it would quench their thirst and keep them alive. He made them rest in the shade by day, and kept them walking. When they couldn't walk, he or Hennu carried them. He never, for a single moment, even *thought* that he could not keep them all perfectly safe, until the help the bear had promised came.

For three days and three nights they went on, with no food but date stones and no water at all.

At dawn on the fourth morning after the eagle had left, Azin heard something. He stopped the song he was singing, put down one of the two children he was carrying (the one who could still walk), and made Hennu stop grumbling.

"What can you hear?" the children asked.

"Voices!" said Azin with a grin.

"Whose voices?" said the children, looking at each other in fear, "We can't hear anything!"

"My brothers!" Azin cried, "And my father! And *all our* camels!"

That's exactly who it was! Ten camels, four brothers, one father and enough water and dates for, well, a very long journey indeed.

That's *almost* exactly who it was, because there was one other camel and one other person. She walked towards them through the haze of dust and light. The children couldn't believe who it was at first. But Azin knew at once, because the birds that had been roosting in her hair took flight, swooping so low over his head that he had to duck.

"Sorry," said the girl, "I was a little lonely without my brothers and sisters. So I asked the birds to keep me company until I found them."

"I thought there wasn't enough honey to break your enchantment?" Azin said.

"Well," said the girl with a shrug, "sometimes good things happen without you expecting them.

Boys with bees, for instance."

"Perhaps," Azin suggested, "our two families can travel together now, then neither of us will ever be lonely."

"Perhaps," replied the girl, "let's see what happens."

And they walked together out of the mountains, while the Enchanted Girl told her story and the Bee Boy listened. Two people, two families, freed by trust and just a little bit of sweetness.

Nicola Davies

Nicola is an award-winning author, whose many books for children include *The Day War Came*, *King of the Sky*, *LOTS*, *Tiny*, *The Promise* (winner of the 2014 English Association Picture Book award for best fiction), *A First Book of Nature* (winner of the Independent Booksellers Best Picture Book), *Whale Boy* (Blue Peter Book Awards Shortlist 2014) and the Heroes of the Wild series (Portsmouth Book Award 2014).

She graduated in Zoology, studied whales and bats and then worked for the BBC Natural History Unit. Underlying all Nicola's writing is the belief that a relationship with nature is essential to every human being, and that now, more than ever, we need to renew that relationship.

Nicola's children's books from Graffeg include *Perfect* (2017 CILIP Kate Greenaway Medal Longlist), *The Pond* (2018 CILIP Kate Greenaway Medal Longlist), the Shadows and Light series, *The Word Bird*, *Animal Surprises* and *Into the Blue*.

Max Low

Max is an illustrator who started work on *Bee Boy and the Moonflowers* whilst still studying illustration at Hereford College of Arts, and has since gone on to work with publishers on further projects, including the picture book series Ceri & Deri, also from Graffeg.

His work draws upon children's artwork and the particularly exciting world of contemporary illustration and design.

Shadows and Light series

The White Hare
Nicola Davies
Illustrated by Anastasia Izlesou

Mother Cary's Butter Knife
Nicola Davies
Illustrations by Anja Uhren

Elias Martin
Nicola Davies
Illustrations by Fran Shum

The Selkie's Mate
Nicola Davies
Illustrations by Claire Jenkins

Bee Boy and the Moonflowers
Nicola Davies
Illustrations by Max Low

The Eel Question
Nicola Davies
Illustrations by Beth Holland

In the days before computers, before cars, before electricity in wires or water in taps, or food in supermarkets, before even roads and writing, people lived by what they could get from the land. Humans were closer to nature, at the mercy of the cold and wind, floods and drought, as other animals were. Back then, humans and animals were fellow beings under the sky. Perhaps that's why it seemed possible, back then, for humans to change into animals, and animals into humans.

A young woman is forced to watch helplessly as a cruel lover slays her family in pursuit of her love.

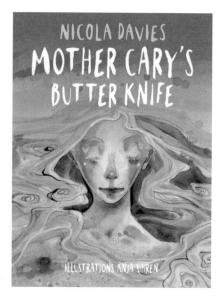

Out of the low slung car a tall, ancient man unfurled himself. His eyes were blue-green, like a backlit wave, his face as craggy as the coast, and topped with a tower of foam-white hair. When the man spoke, his voice was as commanding as storm waves breaking in a cave.

"The sea looks fair tonight, does it not?" he said. Keenan opened his mouth to reply but found his own voice entirely missing. The strange man growled on, and raised a warning finger before the boy's wide eyes.

The smallest of three brothers, Keenan Mowat had a priceless talent: he loved the sea and the sea loved him right back.

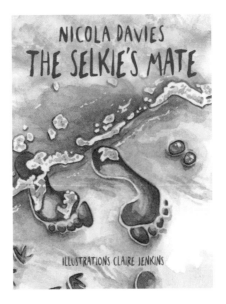

In the far north-west are islands where the sea and land melt into each other in a fretwork of rocks and water. The landscape shifts from liquid to solid in little more than a step. The people who live there shift too, from making a living on land, to the ocean, and back again. Even the seals are not always seals, but sometimes selkies, beings who can slip off their skins to walk on land in human form.

In a land where people flow between ocean and land, a seal and a fisherman sing together under a glowing moon.

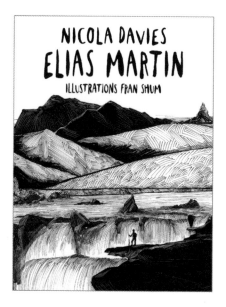

NICOLA DAVIES
ELIAS MARTIN
ILLUSTRATIONS FRAN SHUM

By the time he washed up to the door of a one-roomed log cabin, in the remote backwoods of a northern province, he knew this was his last chance in life. He carried a fur trapper's licence, a bag of steel traps, a rifle and the conviction that all of nature was his personal enemy. He was seventeen years old.

Trawling the north, looking for his last chance of survival, Elias Martin lives a scowling, solitary life for a decade until a small, lost child wanders into his path.

Graffeg Children's Books

The Secret of the Egg
Nicola Davies
Illustrations by Abbie Cameron

The Word Bird
Nicola Davies
Illustrations by Abbie Cameron

Animal Surprises
Nicola Davies
Illustrations by Abbie Cameron

Into the Blue
Nicola Davies
Illustrations by Abbie Cameron

Perfect
Nicola Davies
Illustrations by Cathy Fisher

Small Finds a Home

Celestine and the Hare

Paper Boat for Panda

Celestine and the Hare

Honey for Tea

Celestine and the Hare

Catching Dreams

Celestine and the Hare

A Small Song

Celestine and the Hare

Finding Your Place

Celestine and the Hare

Bertram Likes to Sew

Celestine and the Hare

Bert's Garden

Celestine and the Hare

'Life-affirming books that encourage us all
to nurture the playfulness of childhood'
Playing by the Book